THE LEEDS MURDERS

By
Tony Coleman

CONTENTS

Part 1... 1

Part 2... 4

Part 3... 7

Part 4... 10

Part 5... 12

Part 6... 15

Part 7... 18

Part 8... 21

Part 9... 24

Part 10... 27

Part 11... 30

Part 12... 33

Part 13... 36

Part 14... 40

Part 15... 43

Part 16... 46

Part 17... 49

Part 18... 53

Part 19... 56

Part 20... 59

Part 21... 63

Part 22... 67

About the Author.. 71

PART 1

Jane Wilson was a psychiatrist living and working in Leeds, West Yorkshire.

Jane spends most of her time at work but in the summer she loves to spend her Saturday at Headingley supporting Yorkshire at cricket. Her late father played cricket for many years of his life playing in the Yorkshire league but never reached the level of the county side, a team that consisted of many great players of which many went on to play for England. It was when watching Yorkshire that Jane met Jack Western a police officer who also shared her love of Yorkshire cricket. On the odd occasion Jack would take his wife Mary to the cricket and it was then that he introduced her to Jane who would keep her company while trying to keep one eye on the cricket. Over the years Jane became very good friends with Jack and Mary and they kept in touch throughout the winter when there was no cricket. Jane had spent many years watching Yorkshire and she was featured in the Yorkshire Post many times writing about her love of cricket. Winter was coming to the end and Jane was looking forward to the start of the new season. Yorkshire were at home to Surrey in their opening match and there was sure to be many England players on view. Her friend Jack Western would be there and it would be good to see him again. Mary was not expected to be there as she was a keen gardener and it was also the start of the gardening season. With the first match just a week away Jane looked at her appointment book to see how many people were on her list for the week. Her job gave her the opportunity to finish early on the odd occasion should she need to do so. It was a job that Jane had done for many years, a job she enjoyed and was very good at. People would come to see her with all kinds of problems and she treated each one the same, with kindness, respect and understanding. Jane was also a very good listener which was the number one priority in her work.

The week turned out to be a quiet one with nothing out of the ordinary, but all that was changed when she welcomed her last client for the week. His name was down in the appointment book as Mr. Dixon but when he arrived he introduced himself as Mr. William Morris. Good morning Mr. Morris, I am very pleased to meet you. My name is Jane Wilson and I am a psychiatrist. I understand that you have been referred to me by your doctor under the name of Mr. Dixon. How can I help you today? The man stood in front of Jane looking very smart. He was listed as being 58 years of age but looked much younger. Good morning, he said looking a little nervous, it was good of you to see me so soon. Not a problem said Jane, how can I help. The man smiled and sat down. Would you like a coffee or maybe a tea said Jane. No thank he replied but I would like a glass of cold water if you don't mind. Not at all she said and provided him with a glass of water which he drank immediately. The calmness he had shown when he first arrived was starting to leave him and he was beginning to look very nervous and uneasy.

He looked straight at Jane and said, I am here to see you about the dreams that I get he said, terrible, terrible dreams that scare me to death as they are so real. Can you tell me a little about these dreams Jane said looking straight back at the man? Not sure if I can said Mr. Morris looking more and more nervous, I am trying so hard to block them from my mind. Take your time said Jane, are you sure I cannot get you a tea or a coffee. No thank you he said wiping the sweat from his forehead. I was fine until about a year ago and then I was involved in a road accident while on holiday in Cornwall, spending two days in a coma.

Since the accident I have never been the same person and now I have started having these terrible dreams. Jane could see that her client was starting to get upset and decided that it might be better to end his first appointment. I can see you again next Tuesday afternoon at the same time 3pm if this is suitable for you Mr. Morris. That would be fine with me he replied and he left.

PART 2

Jane was now looking forward to the weekend and Yorkshire playing their first game of the season at home to Surrey. It had been a long winter and Jane was looking forward to seeing her friend Jack Western. The weather was a little on the cool side but then again it usually is in April she thought. The day started bright enough but Jane made sure that she had warm clothing and a flask of hot tea with her. The game started on time with about 4,000 people already in the ground and it was expected to fill up a little more before lunch. Jane was seated in her favourite place and was keeping a look out for her friend Jack. If he was coming to the match, then he always knew where he could find her. The day turned out to be a good one for Yorkshire and when play ended early due to bad light the Yorkshire score had reached 275 for 4 so not a bad start to the season.

Sadly, Jack had not turned up and Jane knew that he must be working. Jack was a police officer working long hours and he often had to work his day off. On her way out of the ground Jane thought she saw another face that she recognised. It was none other than Mr, Morris whom she had seen on the Thursday, the man with the terrible dreams. Later that evening Jane received a phone call from her friend Jack Western to tell her that he had been called away at the last minute and he was very sorry not to have seen her at the match. Jack worked with CID and often had to work his day off, part of the job. Good start for Yorkshire he said to Jane, 275 for 4 against a top side like Surrey was very good. It was a little on the cool side she said but yes your right Jack said Jane it was a good start. Hope to see you at the next game said Jane who could only go on her day off which was a Saturday.

The following week started well for Jane with the news that her sister Mandy was expecting a baby. Mandy and her husband John lived in Thirsk in North Yorkshire. That is good news thought Jane, she was looking forward to being called Aunty Jane. Jane continued with her work then more good news arrived on Tuesday with the news that Yorkshire had just beaten Surrey by 142 runs and had started their season with a big victory. Jack will be so pleased she thought as Surrey are a tough side to beat. Jane picked up her appointment book to see who was next on her list. It was none other than Mr. Dixon or Mr. Morris as he now calls himself. This is the man with the terrible dreams, the same man she had seen at Headingley on Saturday. The appointment was for 3pm and Jane had arranged this time especially, because on his first appointment he got so upset that Jane had to finish his appointment early. This time she was looking to spend a little more time with him. 3pm came and went and there was still no sign of Mr. Morris at 3.30. This man had just wasted 30 minutes of her time and Jane was not very pleased with him. Five minutes later the doorbell rang and in walked a very late Mr. Morris. I am so very sorry he said with a worried look on his face but I got held up with traffic leaving some cricket match. That will be the Yorkshire match with Surrey she said, it ended just after 2pm. I thought I saw you there on Saturday when I was leaving the ground. Never been to a cricket match in my life he said, Football or Rugby is my game. My mistake then said Jane, you must have a double. Please take a seat and we can make a start or would you like a glass of water. Oh yes please he said and Jane poured him out a glass of water which once again he drank instantly. Right said Jane anxious to make a start. These dreams of yours can you tell me anything at all about them and why they are just so hard for you to talk about. Mr Morris was already covered in sweat and he was starting to look a little scared. I just cannot bring myself to talk about them he said, I just want them to go away. I am sorry said Jane but if you cannot tell me anything about them then how can I possibly help you. I do know that he said and I do understand your position and this is why I wrote them down for you. This way you can see for yourself why I am so scared to talk about them, and then next week you can maybe tell me what you think. Once again Jane could see that Mr. Morris was starting to get upset and looked a little scared. She decided on this occasion that he might be right and agreed to read his dreams before his next appointment. Would next Tuesday at 3pm be alright for you Mr. Morris, that's fine he said as he got up to leave. And by the way said Jane, there will be no cricket at Headingley next Tuesday as Yorkshire are playing away from home so please try to be on time as I have other people to see after you. Will do he said, and he left. Jane had a quick look at the notes left by Mr. Morris, the writing was poor and childlike and she decided to read them at home.

PART 3

Jane lived in a small cottage just outside Harrogate. She had lived there since she was a young girl and just loved it. There were plenty of nice walks in the area and it was quiet too which she liked. Her mother had died three years ago and now there was just Jane and her cat Smokey living there. There was a neighbour and friend close by called Eileen who looked after Smokey when Jane was away from home. There were times when Jane would spend the weekend away with her sister Mandy and Eileen had always been there to look after the house and her cat Smokey. After a nice tea and a catch up of the news Jane decided to spend a bit of time reading some of the notes left for her by Mr. Morris and to find out just what he was scared of. The dreams always start in the same way with the capture of a young women who is then pushed into a car and made to drive out into the countryside. She his crying and shouting at the man to let her go. Please let me go she screams, please let me go. I promise I will not say a word to anybody, just please let me out of the car now. The man takes no notice of her, just shut up he shouts, shut up. Your scaring me now she said, I will do anything you ask but please let me go home, my family will be worried about me. Just drive the fucking car the man shouted, drive the fucking car. Eventually they reach the countryside and the man got the woman to drive down a narrow road, then he tells her to stop. No, no, no the girl screams please let me go, please don't hurt me. Where are you taking me she screamed. I was seen getting into your car and the police will find you if you hurt me. Why are you doing this to me, why. Get out of the car the man said and then he starts to drag her to the side of the track. The woman starts screaming again getting louder and louder. The man then punches her in the face, and he puts some kind of tape over her mouth and the screaming stops. The fields at each side of the track were overgrown and covered with brambles and small bushes. It was well away from the main road and unused by anyone. There was no moonlight and it was hard to see anything at all in the darkness. The woman is crying and trying to scream but the tape over her mouth stops her. The man then starts to pull her into the field. She is trying to fight him off and kicking him with her feet. She is terrified at the thought of what this man is going to do with her.

He drags her across the field until he reaches the foundations of what looked like an old farm building. He searches about on the ground until he finds a large stone flag, the flag is very heavy but he still managed to move it to one side, he has obviously been here before. The man drags the woman over to where the flag as been moved, there is a hole in the ground just big enough for one person at a time to get through. He removes the tape from her mouth and gets the woman to sit on the edge with her feet in the hole before putting his foot on her back and shoving her in. The woman is screaming all the time now but there is no one out there to hear her. The man followers her down the hole and shouts at her to stop screaming or he would kill her. She did what he asked, she is now trembling from head to foot and begs him again not to hurt her. The place is cold and damp and the smell just terrible. There are rats everywhere and she could feel them running over her feet. She is terrified and pushes the man away. She starts running down the passage, no one will find you now he shouted, no one will find you now. The woman carried on screaming but only one man would hear her. He removed every bit of his clothing, then put on some kind of a wet suit. He followed the woman down the long narrow passage and it was not long before he found her crouched in a corner. The screaming had stopped and she looked at the man with tears in her eyes. He lifted her to her feet and smiled as he pulled her body towards him. She let out one last loud scream as he thrust a long knife deep into her body. The screaming had now stopped; he had stabbed her many times. She fell to the floor covered in blood, it was everywhere and she was quickly engulfed by rats licking at her blood and feeding on her lifeless body.

PART 4

Jane made a cup of tea and sat down with Smokey her cat who was now sitting on her lap. She felt sick and her thoughts turned back to what she had just been reading. What could I possibly say to this man that would help him to feel better, she had never before been faced in a situation like the one put in front of her by Mr. Morris. The next day Jane returned to work as usual. The sun was shining, the birds were singing and it was good to be alive. The day turned out to be a quiet one for Jane and after seeing her first two clients she decided to phone her sister Mandy who lives in Thirsk, North Yorkshire. Mandy and her husband John were expecting their first child and Jane was excited at being known as Aunty Jane. Mum would have been so pleased she thought. The afternoon came and went with no problems and being such a nice day Jane thought she would go for a walk in the park before heading off home. That evening Jane's thoughts were once more of Mr. Morris and his terrible dreams. Once again she picked up his notes and started to read the second dream which was every bit as terrifying as the first one. Why was this poor man having these dreams which were so graphic and evil? My goodness what more was there to follow. Once more the weekend had arrived and the weather was warm and sunny.

What a pity Yorkshire were not at home today, it would have been nice at Headingley she thought. Yorkshire were playing down at Hove against Sussex and Jane was hoping that the weather would be nice there too. Jane's love of cricket started when she was very young, her father was playing in the local Yorkshire league and Jane's mum went along to help make the tea for the players. Her friend Jack Western was also turning his thoughts to the Yorkshire match at Hove, he too had been a Yorkshire supporter for most of his life. As a young policeman he always put his name down to be on duty at the match.

Jack was due to retire from his job with the police at the end of the following week. I need to ring Jack sometime this week thought Jane and to wish him all the best in his retirement. The soon to be retired officer with a love of Yorkshire cricket would now have time to go to Headingley whenever he wished, or so he thought. Mary his wife had not seen much of her husband due to the long hours he had spent working, but now she could look forward to a bit of help from Jack, but not so much in the garden. Mary spent most of her spare time working in her garden but it was a job that she was happy to do. There were many jobs in the house that needed to be done such as painting and decorating, a job Mary hated doing. Now she was looking forward to handing these jobs over to Jack. There had been many times when Jack had told his wife that he needed to go back to work for a couple of hours in the afternoon. He would ask Mary if she would make him a few sandwiches together with a flask of tea. Mary had not been fooled by this and a quick check outside on the weather confirmed her suspicion that he was heading off to Headingley to watch the cricket. Jack worked hard in his job with the police and spent many hours away from home. Because of this Mary was happy for him to carry out his little plan not knowing that she knew about it.

PART 5

However she did say to him on one occasion that it was always warm and sunny when he needed to go back to work. At the end of the day life was good, Jack was enjoying a little extra time at the cricket watching Yorkshire and Mary was spending her day in the garden. Not long to your retirement now Jack she said, and no longer days away from home. Just think about it Jack said Mary, you can do all those jobs around the house that you promised to do but never found the time. We will just have to wait and see said Jack, I don't want to be doing too much too soon. Yes, quite right said Mary with a smile, you need to take it easy for a week or two and spend a little more time at Headingley. Jack smiled, that's just what he intended to do and Mary knew it. Jane was having a quiet weekend too, she had thought of going into Leeds shopping but then decided against it, the shops are always packed at the weekend anyway she thought. Just then the phone rang, it was Jane's sister Mandy wanting to know if she would like to spend the weekend with her and husband John. Mandy was excited about the baby she was expecting and wanted to talk baby talk with her sister. That would be lovely said Jane, if my neighbour Eileen will feed Smokey I can be with you in a couple of hours. Her neighbour was always happy to feed Smokey and Jane left to visit her sister. The weekend soon came to the end and it was back to work for Jack who was starting his last week with the police. It would be hard for him to say goodbye to a job he had done for many years and there would be a tear or two at the station this week. Jack was also saying goodbye to many of his friends who he had worked with for many years and now it was all coming to the end. Jane too was back at work after spending the weekend with her sister Mandy at Thirsk. Mandy was expecting her first child and she could not wait to become a mum. Jane thought about Jack and she was hoping to see him at Headingley on Saturday when Yorkshire were at home to Middlesex. Later that day Jane received a phone call from Jacks wife Mary to tell her that Jack was hoping to see her at the match. That is good news said Jane, I am really looking forward to it. I see there is still no news about the missing girl Mary said, that's the second girl to go missing in the last two months. It's terrible said Jane, it leaves you scared to go out on your own. Sorry Jane must go, someone at the door. Don't forget Jack will see you Saturday. Jane was quite busy for the rest of the day seeing three more clients before leaving for home at 5.30. On her way home Jane bought the Yorkshire Post as usual and the headline was all about the latest young girl to go missing. The search had now extended into West Yorkshire which worried Jane. I must get home while it is still daylight she thought, it's not safe to be out on your own. That evening Jane watched TV and spent a little time with her cat Smokey who was always glad to see her. I must catch the sports news and see how Yorkshire are doing in their game down at Hove where Yorkshire were playing Sussex, and then it's off to bed. Big day tomorrow she thought, seeing Mr. Morris again at 3pm, I do hope that he turns up on time this week. The next morning Jane looked out from her bedroom window to see heavy rain falling and decided to take a taxi into work. It would be much better than waiting for a bus in this weather. Jane was hoping for much better weather down at Hove where Yorkshire needed just 125 runs on the final day to beat Sussex. The morning passed quite quickly and her thoughts turned to 3pm and her appointment with Mr. Morris. I expect the poor man is worried and not looking forward to our meeting she thought. How wrong she was, Mr. Morris turned up on time and with a big smile on his face too. Nice to see you again he said and shook her hand. I do hope my notes did not scare you too much.

Well said Jane, you were right to say that the dreams were horrible and that they scared you. Looking straight at him she asked if all his dreams were as bad as this one. Afraid so he said, and they all leave me scared and frightened. This is why I do not like to talk about them. Once again Jane could see that he was starting to feel uneasy with sweat starting to appear on his forehead. Jane asked him if he would like a glass of water, yes, please he said and once again drank it in one go. When did you first start with these dreams Jane asked.

It was after my car accident he said and now I get them all the time. I keep a record of all my dreams. I will send another one or two to you so you can read them, then tell me what you think. He was keen for Jane to read more dreams and even seemed excited at the thought. May I have another glass of water please he said, his forehead was covered in sweat. Jane was now having a different view of Mr. Morris, she thought he was sweating because he was excited and not scared. I must go now he said to Jane, I will send you a copy of the dreams in the post. He was shaking Jane's hand and she noticed what looked like a nasty bite mark on his left hand. That looks nasty she said and he quickly pulled away. Shall I see you again next Tuesday. Jane looked at her appointment book for the following week. Yes, that's fine she said, but there is a big match at Headingley where Yorkshire are playing Middlesex so give yourself plenty of time to avoid the traffic.

PART 6

Jane was now finished for the day and decided to leave work early. She stopped for her evening paper and then took a taxi home to her cottage in Harrogate. Jane was greeted at the door by her cat Smokey who could always tell what time of the day it was by his stomach. I must ring Mandy she thought, just to find out how she is. Mandy was Jane's younger sister who lived with her husband John in Thirsk. Her first child was due soon and Jane phoned her almost every day. Mandy was fine, she had her bag packed and was ready to go when the time came. I will ring you every day Jane said, excited at the thought of being called Aunty Jane. After her evening meal and feeding Smokey her cat Jane turned to the back page to read that Yorkshire had beaten Sussex by five wickets and were top of the county championship table. That is good news, Jack will be delighted. The weather the following day was much better. The sun was shining and the birds were singing. Jane had just three people to see in the morning so she arranged to spend the afternoon with Jacks wife Mary who had promised to show her round her beautiful garden. I love my garden she said to Jane, and I would be so lost without it. Jack is just hopeless in the garden, not something he his happy to do. Well he's going to have plenty to do now he is retired said Jane. Mary smiled, he just wants to put his feet up and rest she said, and of course watch plenty of cricket. Have the police had any news on the missing girls yet Jane asked. Don't think so, and Jack has said nothing to me, but then he never does. Your garden is so beautiful said Jane, you must spend lots of time in it to keep it so nice. Its a labour of love dear, and I think the birds appreciate it too as they sing to me all day long. Now, would you like a nice cup of tea or coffee said Mary, or maybe a nice cold drink with it being so warm. A cup of tea would be lovely said Jane. She glanced at her watch, just time for one more walk round the garden Mary then I must be on my way. Thank you so much for taking time to show me your beautiful garden, its been a wonderful afternoon and your garden is a picture, Jack must be so proud of you. The rest of the week was very busy for Jane and she had many more clients to see before the weekend. Jane also phoned her sister Mandy every day just to make sure that she was feeling well and how excited she was about the baby. Saturday arrived and Yorkshire were at home to Middlesex who had also made a fine start to the season. The weather was warm and sunny and Jane was looking forward to a good day's cricket. Jane had also arranged to meet up with Mary's husband Jack Western who had just retired from his job with West Yorkshire Police. Now he had retired he could spend more time at Headingley watching the cricket. When Jack arrived he could see that Jane was already there before him. Jack gave her a big hug, nice to see you again Jane he said with a big smile on his face, hope you are keeping well. I am indeed she said, at the moment I could not be better. My sister Mandy who lives in Thirsk is expecting her first child. I am soon to be Aunty Jane she said smiling. That is good news said Jack, Mary will be so pleased for you when I tell her. How was your week Jack, it must have been so hard for you having to say goodbye to all your friends at the station? It was Jane but we all have to retire at some time and now is the right time for me. Jane smiled at him, you're a man of leisure now and you can do all those jobs around the house that you never had the time to do, so Mary will be delighted. Jack was quick to change the subject back to cricket. Yorkshire have won the toss and decided to bat first he said to Jane. We need a big score to have a chance of beating this lot he said. Middlesex have a very strong team and Yorkshire needed to play well. At lunch Yorkshire had reached 85 for 1 and had made a good start. It's time for our lunch too he said to Jane opening his sandwich box. Let me see what delights Mary has packed for me today, hope it includes a pork pie. Jane started on her lunch too and they both sat in the sunshine enjoying their meal. Have the police had any news on the two missing girls yet asked Jane. Afraid not he said, at the moment the police have no clues at all and nothing to go on. The Lancashire police are now involved too and my friend Bill Rogers is leading investigations. Bill is a big cricket fan too and you will meet him when Lancashire come to Headingley as Bill never misses a roses match. Bill was born in Lancashire but he now lives in West Yorkshire. Play got under way again after lunch with Yorkshire losing two quick wickets. The crowd had grown in size to around 8,000 and they were being treated to some entertaining cricket from both sides. At the end of the first day Yorkshire had taken their score to 275 for 6 with honours just about even.

PART 7

The following day being Sunday and no cricket Jane decided to spend a quiet day at home with her cat Smokey and to read through the Sunday papers. Eileen who was Jane's friend and neighbour popped in for a coffee and a chat and invited Jane to spend a couple of hours with her at the local Antique fair in Harrogate. That would be lovely Jane said, not been there for years. Pick you up in half hour said Eileen, there should be quite a few there today. The Antique fair was packed and you had to fight your way to each stall. Jane was not really interested in Antiques but Eileen bought one or two items. Just as they were about to leave Jane spotted a collection of last year's Wisden cricket magazines which the owner was selling off cheap to avoid having to take them back home. Jane was hoping there would be photographs of Yorkshire players in them and made him a small offer which he was glad to except. I love looking through old cricket magazines she said to Eileen, I must have at least fifty at home. Will you be working Monday Jane or going to Headingley Eileen said? I will be working on Monday she said but I know someone who will be going, she was thinking about her friend Jack Western who had just retired. He was now free to go to Headingley on any day he wanted and Jane knew exactly where he would be on Monday. Jack wanted to take his wife on one of the days but she preferred to stay in her garden. Jane was back at work Monday and her first job was to ring her sister Mandy to ask how she was. I'm fine she said, don't you worry Jane, we will let you know when the baby is due. Make sure you do she replied and returned to her work. Meanwhile Mary had packed a nice lunch for Jack which included a pork pie, and he was off to the game with a spring in his step. Yorkshire and Middlesex were involved in a high scoring game with neither side getting on top. Tuesday morning saw the game heading for a draw so Jack decided to miss the last day of the match and to stay at home with his wife Mary, Yorkshire had a lead of just 28 runs with all their wickets in hand and time was running out for a victory by either side. Tuesday afternoon and Jane Wilson was seeing her last client of the day; it was Mr. Morris the man with the terrible dreams. Jane had read a couple of them and now wanted to find out a little more about the man himself. WHERE HE WORKED.

WAS HE MARRIED. WHAT WERE HIS HOBBIES, was he still having the bad dreams and were they all the same? Also she wanted to know how many hours' sleep did he get following a dream, or was he so scared that he got none. These are the answers Jane was looking for before she could look at ways of helping him. Mr Morris once again managed to arrive on time, looks like I just made it before the end of the game he said, I expect it will get busy in the next hour. Yes, it will said Jane, always busy at the end of the day. Have a seat Mr. Morris, would like a glass of water as usual. Morris smiled, yes please a glass of water would be fine. Right said Jane, this week I want to take it a little further by asking you one or two questions. I want to find out a little about your lifestyle if that's alright with you. Mr. Morris looked nervous but agreed to answer some questions. At the end of the day it might help us in finding out why you're having these dreams she said. At the moment are you in full employment, yes I am he replied and I work for myself as a gardener. And how long have you been doing this job for Mr. Morris she asked. About five years he said, it can be hard work but its a job that I love doing. What about hobbies, you have already told me that you don't like cricket and that rugby and football is your game. Have you any other hobbies that you like. Not really he replied, my work takes up most of my time. What about family, are you a married man or single Mr. Morris. Single he replied quickly and with no plans to marry at the moment. These dreams, are you still having them or have they stopped. I am still having them he said, still the same terrible dreams. Did you receive the ones that I posted to you? I did indeed she replied, in fact I received them this morning. Right said Mr. Morris I have to work this evening so I must get off home early if you don't mind. Not at all said Jane, I will try to read your dream before I see you again next week. Will that be Tuesday at the same time he said, that's right Tuesday 3pm said Jane. There was just one more call to make, and that was to her sister in Thirsk. It was Mandy's husband John who answered the call and he told her that everything was fine, there were no problems and Mandy was resting. Right said Jane tell her that I called and that I will call her again Wednesday morning. Later that evening Jack Western was reading his evening paper. Jack had missed the last day of Yorkshire's match with Middlesex and decided to stay at home with Mary.

The match was heading for a draw and there was no point in watching a game where neither side could win.

PART 8

Mary had spent her day in the garden and had just started to make the tea when there was a knock at the door. Jack was surprised to see it was his old friend from the Lancashire police Bill Rogers. I was in the area so I thought I would pop in and see my old mate now that he has retired. I was just trying to catch up with the latest score from Headingley when you arrived said Jack, but it looks almost certain to be a draw. Well how are things with you Jack said Bill, are you enjoying your retirement, nothing to do and all day to do it in. Jack laughed, I am he said but it is strange not going to the station any more. I will miss my friends, some of which I have known for many years.

Bill works with the Lancashire police but lives in West Yorkshire. He is also a big fan of Lancashire at cricket and sits next to Jack at Headingley when Yorkshire meet Lancashire in a match known as "The war of the roses." Well this is a nice surprise said Jack. Mary look who as come to see us. Oh it's you Bill she said giving him a big hug, come in and sit yourself down. I am just about to make a bit of dinner Bill and your more than welcome to stay and eat with us. That would be nice he said, I am a little hungry and you're such a good cook Mary. Talking of old friends Jack, there are one or two over at the station in Lancashire that want to send you their best wishes, especially sergeant Davies who you know very well. Also Lucy the tea lady who you used to keep busy on all your visits. I did indeed said Jack, she made a grand cup of tea did Lucy. Are you over here on police business Bill or is it your day off today. Although Bill worked over in Lancashire he lived in Leeds. My uncle lives in the area and I have not seen him for a while so I thought I would call in and see you at the same time. Well I am glad you did Bill, it's always good to see you again, especially when Yorkshire are at the top of the table. Bill smiled he knew just how much Jack loved his cricket. Right the both of you said Mary coming out of the kitchen, sit yourself down at the table.

Its not much but it will put you on until you get home Bill. Well it looks and smells nice he said, you're lucky to have married such a good cook Jack. Your quite right replied Jack, I got one of the best when I found my Mary. After a good meal the three of them sat by the fire talking about old times. Still no news about the missing girls then Bill. Nothing at all he said, no clues left and we don't have much to go on at all. I understand another girl has now gone missing, strange that nothing as turned up. The three of them spent the rest of the evening still talking about old times until it was time for Bill to leave. Well it's been nice to see you again said Mary and you must promise to call in again when you're in the area. Yes, I have enjoyed it very much said Jack. Mary is right pop in when you're in the area, your welcome anytime Bill. I promise he said and got up to leave. Almost forgot said Jack, will I see you at the roses match at Headingley this year. Never missed one yet Bill said, with a smile on his face. Its always good to see a Lancashire victory in the roses match. The following day Jack decided to take Mary into Leeds to do a bit of shopping, it was Wednesday and market day so it would be quite busy. Mary was delighted, I never thought I would see the day when Jack Western would find the time to take me shopping.

I thought so too said Jack, maybe this retirement is not so bad after all. Meanwhile Jane Wilson was planning a surprise for Jack at Yorkshire's next home game with Hampshire which was a week on Saturday. Jane had been a Yorkshire supporter for years and she had got to know many of the players. She wanted to ask the Yorkshire captain if he would arrange the signing of a full sized cricket bat by the Yorkshire players and present it to Jack before the start of play. First I must put the idea to Jacks wife Mary and ask her what she thought of the idea. Jane had been kept very busy at work on Wednesday and Thursday but on Thursday evening after a nice tea and a catch up with the Yorkshire match at Leicester Jane decided to read the third dream which Mr. Morris had sent to her by post. If it was anything like the first two dreams which had left her feeling quite sick, then it was not something she was looking forward to reading. First I must ring my sister Mandy and apologise for not ringing this morning. Jane had been ringing every day for the last ten days, and intended to ring every day right up to the baby being born. Mandy was fine and she told Jane not to worry so much. I promise you will be the first to know Jane when the baby is on the way. Jane was happy to hear this and said goodbye.

PART 9

Right, back to Mr. Morris and his dreams. As with the first two dreams a woman was taken captive by a man and shoved into a car. She was asked to drive the car out of town and into the countryside. The woman realised she may be in the hands of a serial killer and starts to blow the horn loud and long trying to catch the attention of any passing motorist. The man becomes angry and strikes the woman across her face with his fist. Shut the fuck up he shouts, or I will kill you here and now. The woman is now terrified and she started shaking, the car was all over the road. She had read the reports in the paper of other women going missing and she knew that she was going to die too. The woman then tried to scare him by telling him that her friend had seen her being pushed into the car and that the police would be out looking for her now. The man takes no notice of what she was telling him. Just drive the fucking car he shouts and I will not hurt you. Her voice was trembling and she thought about her family and started to cry. Once again she screamed, I don't want to die, please just let me out of the car and I will not say anything to anybody. The man started laughing, he was enjoying every minute. Just drive the fucking car he shouted, just fucking drive. After another hour of driving out into the countryside the man told her to stop the car and to switch off the engine. There were no lights anywhere and it was very dark. He looked inside the boot of the car and removed a black plastic bag which he dropped at her feet. Where are you taking me you said you were not going to hurt me. The man is laughing, just pick up the bag and follow me he said. The bag was very heavy and the terrified woman had to drag it behind her. He led her across a field which was very overgrown with brambles, and these were cutting into woman's legs. I have done what you asked she screamed, please, please just let me go, the police will be looking for me. The man started clearing away the brambles until he found a large stone flag. It was very heavy but he was strong and managed to move it with no problems. There was a number of steps leading down into a narrow passage, it was very dark and the smell was terrible. The man shoved the black bag down into the hole and then pushed the woman in after it. She screamed as she fell, falling on top of the black bag. Please let me go she shouted, please let me go. The man took no notice and removed a torch from his pocket asking the woman to empty the bag onto the floor. The woman did as she was told but she could see nothing as it was too dark to see anything. Here you are use this torch he said, tell me what you see. The woman shone the torch on the ground, it was very quiet. Then she saw what was in the bag, and she started screaming louder than ever. The bag contained body parts and lots of them. She ran off down the passage and then fell to the ground, she had fallen over the body of a dead woman being eaten by hungry rats. She was terrified and passed out. Meanwhile the man was changing into a black wet suit before setting off up the passage to find her. She had now recovered from the shock and had realised that she was about to die. There was no way out of the passage and a quick death would be a blessing. She reached the end of the passage and stood with her face to the wall and waited on the man to find her. He was soon standing behind her and once more started to laugh. He put his left arm round her neck pulling her nearer to him. She bit him hard on his left hand as he thrust a knife hard and deep into her back. He stabbed her about twenty times and there was blood everywhere. She fell to the ground in a pool of blood and there were rats licking at her dead body.

PART 10

Jane felt sick, that's the last one she was going to read, and she would tell Mr. Morris that on his next appointment. The weekend arrived and Jane decided to spend a day at York, she had not been there for quite a few years and it would be nice to visit York Minster again. There was still no news from her sister Mandy about the baby so Jane managed to get the next train to York.

The following week the weather was warm and sunny and Jack was quite happy watching his wife at work in the garden. He did however manage to decorate the spare bedroom; a job he had wanted to do for years but never found the time.

Jane was having a busy week and only managed to ring her sister at lunch time.

Mr. Morris failed to turn up for his Tuesday appointment and Jane was not very pleased. He must have had a big gardening job to finish as it was not like him to cancel. Jane was looking forward to Saturday and seeing her friend Jack Western. Jack had recently retired from his job with the police and Jane was planning a little surprise for him. Jane had already told his wife Mary about her idea and she was delighted. A bat signed by the Yorkshire team, Jack would love it she said to Jane. The presentation was due to take place on the field just before the start of Yorkshire's home game with Hampshire. The Yorkshire Post had agreed to cover the story and were sending their reporter. How very exciting thought

Jane. The day of the match arrived and Jane looked out of her window at home just to check the weather. It was warm and sunny and the forecast was good. Jane was delighted, it was just what she wanted for Jacks presentation and she could not wait. Smokey her cat was also up and about early, he wanted his breakfast and then a long sleep after a night on the tiles. Jane arrived at the ground early, she had arranged a meeting with the newspaper reporter and she was also keeping an eye out for Jack who now had to be told about the presentation as he needed to be down on the field just before the start of play.

The reporter and his camera man had to be there too to get a good photograph. The reporter just had time to get a few details from Jack about his retirement and then it was down to the field for the presentation, and a photograph of Jack together with the Yorkshire captain and Jane. After it was over Jack and Jane returned to their seats and Jack could not take his eyes of his signed cricket bat, which was now his prized possession. He could not wait to tell his wife Mary, not knowing that she already knew about it, and that Jane had told her. At the end of the days play Jack rushed out to buy the Yorkshire Post to see if his photograph was on the sports page, but it was not. Try the front page said Jane, and there it was down at the bottom of the page. I don't believe it Jack said, wait while they see this down at the station. And what will Mary and Bill think when they see it. Oh I am pleased for you Jack said Jane, I hope you enjoy your retirement. It was Sunday morning and Jane was thinking back to the day before and Jacks presentation of a signed cricket bat at Headingley. He was so pleased thought Jane, and to see his face when he picked up the Yorkshire Post really was a picture. She made herself some breakfast and a meal for her cat Smokey who was still sleeping in the chair.

29

PART 11

Jane turned to the Sunday papers which had just arrived. There across the front page were the headlines of yet another young woman to go missing in Yorkshire, but this time much nearer to home, the girl came from Leeds, the city where Jane worked. The woman had last been seen in the Bramley area of Leeds late on Tuesday evening, and had not been seen since. The police statement said that it was too early to link the disappearance of this woman with the other missing women in Yorkshire. The police were asking the public for any information that might help them with their enquiries.

Jane read the full report once again, she was shocked to read that this woman had gone missing so near to home. She quickly phoned Jack to ask if he had seen the Sunday papers. Jack laughed, don't tell me I am on the front page of the Sunday paper too Jane. There is another young woman gone missing Jack but this time its much nearer to home. She was last seen in the Bramley area of Leeds last Tuesday and as not been seen since. The police are asking the public for any information that might help them with their enquiries. Tuesday evening, let me see that was the evening that my friend Bill Rogers called to see me. He spent a good couple of hours with myself and Mary. Bill lives in West Yorkshire but works for the Lancashire police in CID. I did ask him if there were any new leads in the case of the missing women and he said there were none. It is so frightening said Jane and I will be so pleased when they catch whoever responsible. Changing the subject, Jane asked Jack if he enjoyed his presentation day at Headingley. Oh I did Jane, it was. one of the best days of my life and I cannot thank you enough. The bat is now my prized possession. I understand that Mary knew about your little surprise too, and now I understand why she made sure that I left home early. Will you be going to Headingley on Monday now your retired Jack? Yes, I am he replied, Mary has some gardening to finish so it works out just right for both of us. The rest of the day Jane spent watching a little TV. Meanwhile Smokey her cat was doing what he likes doing best, sleeping in the chair. The start of a new week and Jane left for work as usual, picking up the Yorkshire Post newspaper on her way. The Yorkshire Post had the story of the missing girl over its front two pages. How many more women would go missing before the person responsible was caught thought Jane, surely somebody knows something that might help the police. Once again Jane managed to leave work early and went home in a taxi. I don't feel safe on my own she thought, and taking a taxi home would be quicker than catching a bus. The weather was once again warm and sunny, and Jack spent Monday and Tuesday at Headingley where Yorkshire managed to beat Hampshire in a very exciting finish. Mary was quite happy in the garden, and it was looking beautiful. When Jack returned home from the cricket Mary asked him if he fancied a couple of days at Whitby. The weather was quite nice and a few days by the sea would do them both good. What a good idea said Jack, that would be a nice change for both of us. The rest of the week turned out to be pretty uneventful for Jane and once again Mr. Morris had to cancel his appointment. Mary and Jack had stayed on at Whitby until Friday morning. I fancy a night out at the pub tonight Jack said Mary I could ring Jane and ask her if she would like to join us, it will do her good to get out a bit more. Jane had joined them at their local before and she had always enjoyed it.

Jane was delighted at the chance of another night out with her two best friends, looking forward to it she told Mary. Jane arranged for Eileen to keep eye on Smokey while she was away and took a taxi to the pub to join up with her friends Mary and Jack. Did you go to Headingley on Monday and Tuesday said Jane.

I did said Jack and what a game it turned out to be, it was good to see a Yorkshire victory after so many draws in the last few games. We have just returned from Whitby this morning after a few days rest by the sea. What about your week replied Jack, anything exciting or was it just the usual problems that your clients turn up with? Well there is one interesting client that I see said Jane. I cannot give out a name for obvious reasons but next time we meet I will tell you a little about him. It's quite horrible really she said but I do not want to spoil our evening. Quite right said Mary, its quiz night tonight and we need to concentrate on winning it.

PART 12

Mary, Jack and Jane enjoyed a nice pub meal washed down with a glass or two of Yorkshire beer. It was not long before the subject turned to cricket and Yorkshire's match with Derbyshire due to start the following day. Meanwhile Mary was doing her best to change the conversation but with little luck. Once again the evening came to a close with the pub quiz, but the three of them were out of luck and finished in third place. Saturday morning the weather was cool but dry and Yorkshire were at home to Derbyshire and a good crowd was expected. Jane was meeting up again with her friend Jack who had already arrived. Morning Jane he said with a smile on his face, it looks like the weather will stay dry today but we could do with some sunshine. Yes, your right Jack she said but the forecast is good for later in the day. Yorkshire had won the toss and decided to bat first hoping to get a good start on the first day. Once again there were quite a few International players on view and the crowd was building up quite nicely. Oh Jack said Jane, I had such a wonderful night last night at your local pub. It was good of both yourself and Mary to invite me out with you once again. I enjoyed the quiz, even though we only came third. I am already looking forward to the next night out she said. You know you are always Welcome anytime. and in any case we need you for the quiz. I want a word with you at lunch Jack if you don't mind. I promise not to take up too much of your time.

Not a problem said Jack and they both settled down to watch the mornings play. Lunch arrived with the Yorkshire score on 75 for 1. Mary had packed a nice lunch again for Jack which also included a small pork pie which Jack was very fond of.

First of all, I have some very good news, I received a phone call from my sister Mandy this morning to say that she has given birth to a baby girl just after midnight. I am so excited Jack, and now I am Aunty Jane. I am going to see her first thing Sunday morning. That's wonderful news said Jack, Mary will be so pleased when I give her your news. Have they given the little girl a name yet?

I think it might be Lucy or Jean but all that could change. My mother's name was Jean so that would be nice. Now Jane what was it you wanted to talk to me about.

I will then do my best to help if I can. Jane looked quite serious and started to tell Jack about her client Mr. Morris and his horrible dreams. She told Jack about the last dream where the woman had to drag a bag of body parts across a field and ended up being eaten by hungry rats. My god said Jack. That really is a terrible dream, and you say he keeps having these dreams. Yes, that's right said Jane. He tells me that he is so scared to talk about them yet he looks to be enjoying it when he gets me to talk about them. The man scares me she said and I do not trust him at all. I have seen him at Headingley but he told me that he has never been there. I asked him what his job was and he told me that he was a gardener, but his hands are cleaner and softer than mine and not the hands of a gardener. He told me that he first started having these dreams after a car accident had left him in a coma, he went to see his GP who then referred him to me. Every time he talks about his dreams he quickly starts to sweat and keeps asking for water. I think that be enjoys it when he sees how uneasy I get just talking about them.

I don't want to see him again and Tuesday will be his last appointment with me. I am scared Jack, really scared. Well I am glad you're going to refer this man back to his doctor Jane especially if he scares you. Will you be alright on your own next Tuesday or would you prefer it if someone was with you. I will be alright on my own Jack but I will be glad when he has gone. The rest of the day went well, the sun came out and Jack and Jane were both enjoying the cricket. Jane went home from the game feeling much better now that she had told Jack about Mr. Morris and now her thoughts turned to the new baby. With Smokey sat on her lap Jane thought about the little girl and what they were going to call her. I do hope its Jean; mum would be so proud to have her granddaughter named after her. On Sunday morning Jane left early to visit Mandy, husband John and the new baby, she intended to stay for most of the day and she was very excited. Mary and Jack spend their Sunday with a day in the Yorkshire Dales, it was always beautiful there at this time of the year and they both loved every minute. Now your retired Jack we should spend a week here and its not too far from home. Your quite right Mary and we will do that he said.

PART 13

It was soon the start of another new week and a very happy Jane returned to work after spending a wonderful day with her sister and the new baby over in Thirsk. Mandy and husband John had decided to call the new baby girl Lucy and Jane was so happy. Mary made up a packed lunch for Jack who was heading off to Headingley for the cricket, I must remember a small pork pie she thought, and a nice cool drink as the weather is warm and sunny today. Meanwhile Mary had planned a nice long day in the garden which is where she wanted to be. The flowers were all in bloom and the birds were singing, she could not think of a better place to be. Tuesday was also a warm and sunny day and once again Jack was heading to Headingley for the final day of Yorkshire's game with Derbyshire. Mary had planned a coffee morning with her neighbour Jean who had just returned from a two weeks' holiday in Scotland and wanted to tell Mary all about it. Meanwhile Jane Wilson had a busy day in front of her which included another appointment with Mr. Morris who had cancelled his appointment the week before due to working late. Jane had read the latest dream sent to her by Mr. Morris which turned out to be more gruesome than the previous two and Jane had felt quite sick after reading it. Mr. Morris arrived on time 3pm despite the Yorkshire match and before the crowd had started to leave. After a quick handshake he took his seat and immediately apologised to Jane for missing his appointments. I really am sorry about last week he said but once again the job I was doing took longer to finish than 1 thought. Jane noticed how clean and soft his hands were, not the hands of a hard working gardener. Mary was always telling her that gardening gave her problems with her hands leaving them dry and hard. Have you had time to read the last dream that I posted to you he asked. I have replied Jane and I must say it was by far the most frightening dream of all. That would be the dream with the black bag and the body parts he said. One again Jane noticed how pleased he looked when she discussed his dreams. Yes, that's the one she said and I was shocked that anyone could have such an evil dream. Once more Morris was starting to sweat heavily and was quick to ask Jane for a glass of cold water. Jane had seen this look before and was starting to feel uneasy about carrying on. The weather has been warm again today said Jane trying to change the subject for a minute or two. I expect this is your busy time of the year. Yes, I am quite busy at the moment he said, very busy indeed. Have you asked your doctor about sleeping tablets said Jane? If you're working quite hard then you need a good night's rest. Jane ended the thirty-minute appointment and prescribed a week's supply of a mild sleeping tablet. I will see you again next Tuesday at the same time 3pm Mr. Morris if this is convenient with you. Should you need to cancel please let me know the day before, then I can rearrange my appointments.

That's fine he said and apologised again for his missed appointment in the previous week. Jack and his wife Mary were enjoying a nice evening meal.

Jack had spent the day at Headingley where he saw Yorkshire beat Derbyshire by 78 runs to go top of the table again. After their meal Mary decided to do a bit of dead heading on her roses while Jack had a sleep in his chair. I expect you are looking forward to the next Test match Mary said giving Jack a tap on the head. England against Australia at Headingley. Yes, quite right said Jack jumping up from his chair, what was that you were saying. Oh Jack said Mary with a smile on her face, did I wake you. Sorry about that said Jack, but I do tend to nod off when I see you working in the garden. Yes, I know you do said Mary, I can hear you Jack. Anyway what were you saying Mary. I was just saying Jack that it's the Test match a week on Thursday at Headingley, England v Australia. Yes, your right Mary and if the weather stays like this it will be a full house on most of the five days. This is why I booked our tickets as soon as they went on sale. Will Jane be going too she asked? Yes, Jane will be there on the first four days he said, but she will be back at work on the Tuesday which is a pity as it's the last day of the match. At the end of the week Mary phoned Jane to ask her if she would like to join her and Jack again at their local pub on Friday night. The last time Jane joined them they had a wonderful night and managed to come third in the quiz. Jane was delighted to get the chance to join them again, and she arranged to meet up with them again at their local pub. Jane had a word with Eileen her neighbour asking if she would pop in and check on Smokey While she was away. Jane loved her cat very much and so did her neighbour who was always ready to look after him whenever Jane was away. Jane phoned her local taxi service and set off to join her two good friends Mary and Jack Western who had been regulars at their local pub for many years. It was a small but friendly pub and everybody was made welcome. Jane herself had only been there two or three times but already felt at home. She was looking forward to a nice pub meal and a glass or two of good Yorkshire beer. It was also quiz night and the three of them were determined to win it after finishing third last time. I was looking forward to this evening she said to Mary, it's been a long day and it will do me good. It certainly will say Jack finishing off his pint, who wants another beer.

PART 14

The evening went well but sadly they came only fourth in the quiz. Almost forgot said Jack, we should have one or two Yorkshire players in the England team with Yorkshire being top of the league and the match being played at Headingley. Yes, your right said Jane it makes you so proud to be a Yorkshire cricket supporter. There are quite a few players good enough to make the England team and we should get to know this Sunday when the team will be named. What time will you and Mary be there on the first day Jack as there will be long queue's outside the ground. Yes, I had thought about this Jane and I do not like the idea of Mary standing for such a long time so I thought that if we arrived at 9am the queue might not be so long. We can always read the morning papers, and have a coffee or two and enjoy the morning sunshine. That sounds fine with me Jack and I must remember to pay you for the tickets. I must go now as my taxi will be waiting. Thank you both so much for another wonderful evening. There was a loud sound of a car horn, that will be my taxi said Jane, night all. Yorkshire had no match at the weekend so Jane decided to spend the weekend with her sister Mandy in Thirsk. It would be nice to see little Lucy for a couple of days instead of just a couple of hours. Mary and Jack decided on a quiet weekend, just the two of them enjoying their beautiful garden. On Sunday afternoon Jack caught up with the sports news and the England team, there was just one Yorkshire player in the squad which Jack thought was a big disappointment. On Monday Jane returned to work hoping that the weather would stay warm and sunny for the Test match starting on the Thursday. Jane was also surprised that there was only one Yorkshire player in the team, it was not what she expected. I must remember to pack some nice sandwiches she thought. The queue's at Headingley for food and beer would be long, especially with there being a large crowd. I must also remember my sun cream if it's going to be hot. Eileen her neighbour had agreed to look after Smokey while she was away, I don't know what I would do without her. Jane decided to ring Mary to thank her and Jack for the wonderful night out on Friday. Jack answered the phone as Mary was working in the garden. I am glad you enjoyed your evening out said Jack, you know you are always welcome at any time. I forgot to ask you Jane, are you still seeing this man with the terrible dreams, the one who was starting to scare you.

I am indeed said Jane. I think that I need to know more about the man himself before I make out my report. I am not due to see him again now until the last day of the Test. He phoned up first thing this morning to cancel tomorrow due to working late again. Anyway I must go Jack, love to Mary and I will ring you again on Wednesday just to confirm our meeting on Thursday morning. Jack returned to the garden with a cold drink for Mary who was working away in her garden as usual. That was Jane on the phone he said, she sends her love. She was phoning to thank us both for inviting her to spend Friday evening at our local pub. That was nice of her Jack, Jane is always so grateful to spend time with us, she must get lonely living out in that little cottage with just her cat Smokey and having just one neighbour nearby. Morning said a voice both Jack and Mary knew very well, it must be nice when all you have to do all day is to sit out in the sun with a cold drink and the morning papers. It was the voice of their friendly postman with a large brown envelope addressed to Jack Western. I expect you will be sitting in another place on Thursday he said to Jack with a smile on his face. What about you Mary, will you be going to the Test match too. We are both going said Jack, I have been looking forward to this match for months. I booked tickets for myself and Mary as soon as they went on sale. Yes, it's a sellout said the postman and it's about time we beat the Aussies at cricket too. The weather is beautiful now and the first four days of the Ashes games are usually a sellout. They are said Jack, and with a Yorkshire player in the team it makes it a little more interesting. Anyway if I don't see you both before Thursday, enjoy the cricket and let's hope we can win back the Ashes and quieten the Aussies a bit. Excuse me Mary but we have one or two of them at work and when it comes to cricket they can be a bit of a pain in the backside. I know what he means said Jack. They love to tell us Poms just how good they are at cricket. Maybe a victory for England will shut them up for a year or so.

PART 15

Jack started to open his mail. No idea what this could be he said to Mary, certainly not expecting anything as big as this. Its printed "PLEASE DO NOT BEND" across the front which makes it even more interesting. Jack quickly removed the items from the envelope and to his surprise found three large photographs showing the presentation made to him by the Yorkshire cricket captain of a full sized cricket bat which had been signed by the Yorkshire team. There was a note inside which read "WITH BEST WISHES FROM THE YORKSHIRE POST" That's wonderful said Jack, what a nice surprise, that's just made my day. Mary decided to have two of the photographs framed. There would be one for Jack and she thought it would be nice to have one done for Jane. After all it was Jane who planned and arranged the presentation for Jack with the Yorkshire captain. Mary phoned her local photograph shop asking if they would do the framing for her, framed and ready to pick up on Friday. She thought it would be a nice surprise for Jane, and to hand it to her on Friday or Saturday at Headingley. What a nice idea Mary, Jane will be delighted. It was Thursday and the start of the third Test match between England and Australia at Headingley, Leeds. Jane was up and about early to check on the weather. It was a beautiful morning, warm and sunny with just a slight breeze. There were sandwiches to make up together with a large flask of tea, and a chocolate biscuit or two. She thought about a brolly but then changed her mind as it would take up too much room and the forecast was good. Right I must feed Smokey now and then check with Eileen about feeding him again later in the day if he was hungry.

Then I need to think about my taxi as I don't want to be late on the first day.

The match was a sellout crowd and like Jane people would be heading to the ground early. Jack and Mary had arranged to meet up with Jane at 9am which turned out to be the right thing to do as the crowd was already building up. There she is shouted Jack, over here Jane he shouted. Jane looked glad to see them and made her way across. I see you have a gardening magazine under your arm Mary said Jane. Something for you to read if you need a break from the cricket. Yes, I do like my gardening magazines she said and we still have a couple of hours to pass before the match starts. What about you Jack, have you got your morning papers as usual. I have indeed he replied, as well you know I like to do the crossword. Scorecards a voice shouted, move along please shouted another as the three of them made their way into the ground. England had won the toss and decided to bat first. The weather was beautiful as the England openers walked out to bat first. The large crowd were hoping that England would get off to a good start but all that was forgotten when Archer took the wickets of Richardson, Cowdrey and Oakman, and England were reduced to 17 for 3. The large crowd were sitting in silence until a partnership between Peter May and Cyril Washbrook lifted the England score. Jack, Jane and Mary were loving every minute of it and the day got better with England finishing on 204 for 4 with Cyril Washbrook not out 90. The following day Friday, and the second day of the Test match. Once again Jack and Mary met up with their good friend Jane at 9am and made their way into the ground before the crowd started to build up. The first four days of the match were sold out so you needed to be there early just to avoid the queues.

After a nice cup of coffee Mary removed a parcel from her bag and handed it to Jane. We thought you would like this Jane to remind you of the day Jack received his signed cricket bat from the Yorkshire captain at Headingley. Jane was almost in tears, oh Mary she said, what a wonderful gift you have given me and it will always remind me of our happy days spent at Headingley. We should be thanking you Jane replied Mary, it was your idea to do the presentation to Jack on his retirement. The start of play saw England lose a quick wicket when Cyril Washbrook fell just two runs short of his century when he was out LBW to Benaud. England were now 226 for 5 and Shortly after these two more quick wickets fell, and England were in a spot of trouble at 248 for 7. Insole and Evans then pushed the England score past the 300 mark and they were eventually all out for 325. Australia went into bat and were soon in deep trouble losing their first wicket for just ten runs. This is a good start for England said Jack and it's a Yorkshire man that takes the wicket too.

PART 16

Jane decided to buy the evening paper which were available at the ground. She first turned to the back page to catch up with Yorkshire's match at Leicester.

She then turned to the front page with the headlines "ANOTHER WOMAN MISSING IN YORKSHIRE" the three of them were shocked at the news that a woman had gone missing while walking her dog in Bradford. It was then back to the cricket and England ended the day well on top after taking six Australia wickets for just 81 runs, with both Lock and Laker doing the damage. Mary, Jack and Jane sat in the ground enjoying yet another cup of coffee and happy that England were well on top in the match. After a while the conversation changed to the missing woman in Bradford, how many more women have to go missing before the person responsible was caught said Jane. I am scared to leave the house she said and now travel to work, then back home again by taxi. The police don't have any leads so far said Jack but one day soon they will make a mistake and the police will get the person or person's responsible. Saturday morning and the third day of the Test match, Jane looked out of her bedroom window to check the weather. It was not looking good and the rain was falling quite heavily. She decided to wait a little longer before phoning Jack and Mary to ask what they intended to do. There would be no point going to Headingley until the weather got better and the rain had stopped. Meanwhile Jack and Mary were also disappointed with the weather and like Jane saw no point in going to the ground.

Why don't you phone Jane and ask her if she would like to spend the day with us said Mary? Good idea said Jack then we can all go to Headingley together if the weather gets any better. At that moment the phone rang, it was Jane asking about their plans for the day. I was just about to ring you said Jack, Mary would like to know if you would like to spend the day with us, or at least until we find out what the weather is going to do. That's a good idea said Jane, tell Mary I would love to spend the day with you both. I just need to tell my neighbour to keep an eye on Smokey then I will be straight over. It was still raining hard when Jane arrived and Mary decided to make sandwiches and soup for lunch. I don't hold out much hope for any play today said Jack looking out of the window. The weather is worse now than it was this morning. The ground will be saturated by now. I might be with you on the last day after all said Jane. Mr. Morris has cancelled again and if I can rearrange my other morning appointments then I can join you both at Headingley. That is good news said Jack, if there is no play today then the match will be decided on the last day which is Tuesday. Have you decided where to hang your framed photograph yet Jane said Mary. I have indeed replied Jane; it will hang with pride on my office wall where everyone will see it. Jack picked up his morning papers which had just arrived late due to the bad weather. The story of the missing girl in Bradford was on all the front pages. Somebody must know something about these missing girls Jack said Jane. I cannot understand how four women can simply disappear into thin air without leaving some kind of a clue. The police don't have anything Jane, I was talking to my friend Bill Rogers on the phone only last night and he confirmed that the police had nothing to go on. The day's play was eventually called off for the day at 3pm due to persistent rain and a very wet out field. With England in a very strong position it was hoped that

Sunday would be a sunny day and that play would start on time on Monday morning. Jane decided to head of home before it started getting dark and to spend some time with her cat Smokey who had not seen much of her for a day or two. I will see you both on Monday morning Jack she said as she got into her taxi. We will just have to hope that the weather will be kind to us and that play will start on time.

PART 17

Today has been such a disappointment said Mary, we were all looking forward to another warm day sat in the sun. Your quite right said Jack, the only people who are not so disappointed will be the Australian team and their supporters. Sunday turned out to be a much better day with plenty of warm sunshine and a light breeze. Just the weather we wanted said Jack, this should help to dry out the field of play after all that rain we had yesterday. England are in a very strong position to win the match and square the series at 1-1 so it's vital that play will start on time. With the weather being so nice Mary decided to do a few jobs in the garden while Jack decided to spend a few hours in his chair reading the Sunday papers which had just arrived. He was hoping there might be some news about the missing girls but there was nothing at all. Would you like a nice cup of tea before I start work in the garden said Mary. That would be lovely said Jack, and maybe a chocolate biscuit too, just to put me on until lunch time. Jane was spending her Sunday relaxing too.

She phoned her sister Mandy in Thirsk to ask how baby Lucy was, and she was fine. I will try and get over soon said Jane, I need to keep eye on my little niece.

The rest of the day she spent reading all the Sunday papers and playing with Smokey her cat. Monday morning saw the sun shining and it was quite warm. The news from Headingley was good and play would start on time. Mary and Jack were due to meet up with Jane again at 9am and all three of them were looking forward to a full day's cricket. Australia were starting the day at 81 for 6 and were in big trouble England needed to win this match to square the series at 1-1.

The day went England's way with Australia all out in their first innings for just 143 and trailing England by 182 runs. The England captain enforced the follow on and at the end of the fourth days' play Australia were 93 for 2 and still 89 runs behind. Mary, Jack and Jane all went home happy and were already looking forward to Tuesday and an England victory. Jane had rearranged a couple of her appointments to later in the week and with Mr. Morris having cancelled his Tuesday appointment this left Jane free to join her friends on the final day. Yet another warm and sunny day saw Australia needing to bat all day just to save the match. It was not to be and Lock and Laker ripped their way through the Australian team and they were all out for just 140. England had won the match by an innings and 42 runs to square the series at 1-1 with two to play. The game ended much sooner than many expected so they sat in the sun reading their newspapers and eating their packed lunch. England needed another 8 wickets at the start of play and many thought that the game would last well into the afternoon. Mary, Jack and Jane tucked into their lunch and Mary had included a pork pie for Jack which always put a smile on his face. After a while the three talked more about the missing women. Who was responsible for their disappearance and why were their no clues. It makes you scared to leave the house said Jane, and living on my own leaves you frightened to fall asleep. Why don't you come and stay with us for a week or two said Mary, we have plenty of room and you be very welcome. Yes, why not said Jack, much better than being out there on your own. I would love to said Jane but I have Smokey my cat to think about and it would not be fair to keep asking my neighbour to look after him.

She already spends more time with Smokey than I do. Right time to go said Jack, don't forget Jane, if you change your mind your very welcome to stay with myself and Mary.

Wednesday morning and the first day back at work for Jane following her few days off to see the whole of the Test match between England and Australia at Headingley. It had been a wonderful match for England and their supporters beating the Australians and Jane and her friends Jack and Mary Western had enjoyed every minute. Jane displayed her Yorkshire Post photograph showing the bat presentation to her friend Jack proudly on the wall behind her office desk where it would be seen by everyone. Jack had just retired from his job with the police and it was Jane who arranged for a bat signed by the full Yorkshire team to be presented to Jack by the Yorkshire captain. Before the end of the week the photograph had attracted quite a lot of attention from her clients who had been quick to recognise the Yorkshire captain. The weekend was here again and Yorkshire were once more playing away from home, this time down in Canterbury where they were playing Kent. The victory in their last match over Leicestershire had sent Yorkshire back to of the county championship table and both Jack and Jane were delighted. Aunty Jane as she was now called by her family wanted to spend more time with her niece Lucy, so she arranged to visit her sister in Thirsk and spend a few hours with them.

Mum would be very proud Mandy, baby Lucy is a beautiful little girl and I am so happy for you and for John. Jane was very happy, she had just seen England thrash the Aussies, Yorkshire were top of the table and there was a new member of the family with the arrival of baby Lucy. Mary and Jack were having a quiet weekend at home with Mary spending her time in the garden and Jack resting in his chair reading the morning papers, with a continuous supply of coffee and biscuits. The national newspapers were all covering the disappearance of the missing women in Yorkshire with police still saying there were no leads as to where the women might be. The new week started with Yorkshire back on top of the county championship table and their game down in Kent was also going their way. On Saturday Yorkshire had bowled out Kent for just 118 runs and in reply had finished the day on 156 for 1 with a lead of 38 runs and 9 wickets in hand. Yorkshire's next home game starting Saturday was the roses match with Lancashire. This game always attracted a large crowd and both Jack Western and Jane were looking forward to it being another exciting game.

PART 18

Jack had promised to introduce Jane to his friend and former work colleague Bill Rogers who was a big Lancashire supporter and had never missed a roses match in the last ten years. Bill was working with the Lancashire police on the case of the missing women. The weather was warm and sunny and Jack and Mary decided to spend a few days at Scarborough. They had spent most of their holidays there and always had a good time. It should be nice at this time of the year said Mary and the sea air will do us both good. Jack smiled, there is also a very nice fish and chip shop just across from the harbour he said, with a nice pub next door. Back in Leeds Jane had a very busy week in front of her which included another appointment with Mr. Morris on Tuesday. Jane was not looking forward to the appointment and had decided to end his visits. The week continued with warm weather and Jane spent the evening sat outside her cottage or going for a walk with her neighbour Eileen. Tuesday morning Jane left for work in a taxi and decided to put her appointment with Mr. Mr Morris to the back of her mind until 3pm. After lunch Jane just had the time for a quick phone call to her sister before Mr. Morris arrived. He apologised once again for the cancellation of his appointment the previous week. The weather was so nice I decided to work late each night he said. Jane was surprised to see just how pale he was looking and once again she had her suspicion of him not being a gardener. Would you like a drink said Jane as he took his seat. That would be nice, its so warm out there, a glass of cold water would be fine. Jane turned to get the water and Mr. Morris noticed the photograph on Jane's wall. Would that be you on the photograph he said, I have not seen this before. Would you mind if I take a closer look? Not at all said Jane surprised that he was taking so much interest in the cricket photograph. He had already told Jane that he was not interested in cricket so why the sudden interest now. Who are the other people in the photograph he asked, are they all cricket friends of yours? The one presenting the bat is Billy Sutcliffe the captain of Yorkshire and the other one is my good friend Jack Western who as just retired from the police force. Jack like me is a big supporter of the Yorkshire team and I thought it would be nice to ask the Yorkshire captain to present him with a full sized cricket bat signed by all the players. That is a good idea he said, no doubt your friend was delighted with his gift. Right said Mr Morris getting to his feet. The reason I am here today is to tell you that, at last my dreams have stopped and thanks to you I am now getting a good night's sleep. I am sorry to leave you so quickly but once again I must get back to my job. Jane was both shocked and surprised at Mr. Morris leaving so quickly but she was also pleased that she was never going to see him again. Later that evening Jane fed her cat Smokey and looked at the Yorkshire Post for news on Yorkshire's match down at Canterbury and it was good news. Yorkshire had beaten Kent by 10 wickets and remained at the top of the championship table. Yorkshire next match was the home game with Lancashire at Headingley which was known as the battle of the roses. Jane thought about her friends Jack and Mary who were spending a few days at Scarborough, the weather was nice and sunny so it should be beautiful there at this time of the year. Her friend and neighbour Eileen popped in for a coffee and asked Jane if she would like to have dinner with her on Wednesday evening. It would be nice to catch up on all the news she said and you can tell me about your sister Mandy and her new baby. I will indeed said Jane, my new niece is called Lucy and I am now Aunty Jane, she said with a big smile on her face. Jane watched a little television with Smokey on her lap before going to bed, it had been a long day. The following day Jane made out her report on Mr. Morris and sent it off to his doctor. There was another long day in front of her and her next appointment had already arrived. Meanwhile Mary and Jack were enjoying the sunshine at Scarborough on the Yorkshire coast. The seaside resort was packed due to all the warm weather, blue sky, and plenty of fresh air. This is just what we wanted said Jack, all we are short of is a cricket match.

PART 19

At the end of another busy day Jane was looking forward to sharing a meal with her friend and next door neighbour Eileen who wanted to know all about Mandy and her new baby. After a nice meal and a long chat, the talk turned to the four missing women and how there was still no news from the police. I am so scared said Jane, I do not like to go out on my own and I even take a taxi to work and then back home again. Eileen agreed with her and both women were scared to be out after dark on their own. The rest of the week passed quickly and Jane was already thinking about Saturday and the big roses match between Yorkshire and Lancashire. Jack Western and his wife Mary had returned from Scarborough and Jack would be meeting Jane on Saturday morning. The game always attracted a large crowd and it was always best to get there in good time. Jack had promised to introduce Jane to his friend Bill Rogers who never missed a roses match. Bill was a big Lancashire supporter who lived in Leeds but worked for the Lancashire police. The morning was warm and dry and Jack was looking forward to spending a good day at the cricket with two of his best friends. I have packed you a nice lunch said Mary and a bit extra for Bill just in case he forgets as usual. There is also a flask of tea which should be enough for both of you although I know Bill only likes to drink water. I thought with it being such a nice day I would spend my time in the garden which could do with a bit of a tidy up. Right my love, I must dash, with it being such a beautiful day there is sure to be a large crowd. Jack kissed his wife goodbye and set off on his way to Headingley.

Morning Jack said a voice he knew well, no need to guess where you are going today. It was his local postman who together with half the village knew of Jacks love for cricket. Mary's garden always looked a picture, and she decided to do a little dead heading on her roses and to look for any weeds that dared to show their heads. There would also be time for a coffee and a chat with her neighbour, Jean Richards who also shared her love of gardening. There were many days when the two could be seen in each other's garden exchanging plants. The afternoon passed quickly and Mary must now turn her thoughts to Jack and his tea. With all that fresh air he was bound to be hungry and looking forward to his tea. Jack was always happy with whatever Mary put in front of him providing it included apple pie and custard. Later that day when Jack returned from the cricket with a big smile on his face Mary knew at once that it must have been a good day for Yorkshire, and it had. Bowled them out for just 148 he said and the crowd were delighted, well at least the white rose supporters were. Then the day got even better when Yorkshire ended the day on 175 for 2. oh I am so pleased for you Jack said Mary and it's been such a beautiful day for you too. Mary told Jack about her day in the garden and just how beautiful it was looking. I noticed it when I got back he said, it looks a picture, but then it always does Mary and I am so proud of you. I wish I could do more to help in the garden Mary but I am not much good at it as you already know. Quickly changing the subject from gardening to food, all this fresh air as made me hungry said Jack, what's for tea Mary, I'm starving. Well it's been such a warm day I thought I would do a nice salad but don't worry, there will still be apple pie and custard to finish with.

Did Bill Rogers turn up for the game Jack, and did he meet Jane. No Bill never turned up, it was unusual for him to miss the start of the roses match, very strange. Jane sends her love and is looking forward to another night out at our local pub. Not a problem said Mary, Jane is always welcome anytime. After a good day at Headingley with her friend Jack Western Jane was planning a quiet Sunday morning, reading the morning newspaper and spending a little more time with her cat Smokey. It had been a busy week for Jane who had not seen much of her cat other than to feed him. The Sunday papers all covered the story of the missing women in Yorkshire but police were still saying nothing Jane decided it was best to carry on with her taxi to work, and home again, she was worried about being out on her own. Later that morning Jane phoned Mary to ask about their short holiday in Scarborough, and then phoned her sister Mandy to ask about baby Lucy. The following day Jane left for work as usual in her taxi. The sun was shining and her thoughts had turned to the roses match at Headingley and her friend Jack Western who had recently retired from the police force. Jack was now free to watch Yorkshire on any day that he wanted and Jane was thinking just how lucky he was.

PART 20

Within minutes of arriving at work Jane received an unexpected call from the doctor she had written to just a few days before regarding Mr. Morris. The doctor informed Jane that he had no record of a Mr. Morris ever being referred to see Jane. There had been a Mr. Dixon but his appointment was later cancelled and a letter had been sent out to Jane. Jane was shocked to hear this and became very upset at the thought of this man coming to see her without first seeing his doctor. There had been times when Jane had been scared of this man and she started to cry. Who was this man and why was he going to see Jane and telling her such horrible dreams? Jane cancelled all her appointments for the next two days and decided to ring her friend and former police officer Jack Western. Jack was due to go to Headingley for the second day of the roses match and Jane said that she would meet him there. The crowd at Headingley was starting to build up quite quickly. It was another warm sunny day and Yorkshire were in a very strong position. On Saturday Yorkshire had bowled out Lancashire for just 148 and ended the day on 175 for the loss of just two wickets. Jane arrived to find Jack was already in his seat and he could see straight away that Jane was looking very upset. She told him about the phone call from the doctor and how this man had been seeing her without first seeing his doctor. He had scared her with his terrible dreams and she wanted to know why. Jack promised to ring the station at lunch time and to ask if this man calling himself Mr. Morris was known to the police. If Bill Rogers turns up today we will have a word with him too Jane, although with Yorkshire being well on top! doubt if he will show up. Jack was a former police officer with CID in West Yorkshire and he had been having his own suspicions about Mr. Morris from the day Jane first told him that he was starting to scare her. At lunch Jack made his call to the station and inquired about William Morris but he was not known to police in Yorkshire. Leave it with me he said to Jane. My friend Bill Rogers works with the Lancashire police and I will ring him tonight when I get home. I am so sorry Jack said Jane, I don't want to spoil your day's cricket at Headingley. From now on we will just concentrate on the cricket. Yorkshire were having a good and had reached 268 for 6 at lunch. The afternoon session started well for Lancashire taking the last four Yorkshire wickets for just 23 runs. runs. All out for 291 Yorkshire had a lead of 143. Jane had arrived at the ground with no food or drink but Mary had made sure that Jack would not go hungry so there was plenty for Jack to share. At the end of play Lancashire were 120 for 4 and still 23 runs behind Yorkshire, and victory was in sight for the home side. Why Don't you stay with us for a few days said Jack, Mary would love to see you and your always welcome at any time. I would love to Jack, I really would but I need to be home to look after Smokey. The following day Jane phoned Jack to say that she would be at Headingley for the final day of the roses match. Yorkshire were well on top and it was hard to see how Lancashire would get back into the game. When Jack arrived at the ground he could see once more that Jane was still upset. Did you phone your friend Bill last night Jack? I did he replied, and he was very interested in what I had to say and concerned about the way this man used you for his own enjoyment. He promised to get back to me if the Lancashire police had any information on William Morris. Did you not have the address for this man Jane. I did, but when I checked it out and it turned out to be false. Right Jack, thank you for all your help but now its time for you to enjoy the cricket.

I even made myself a packed lunch today too. Once more the morning was warm and sunny but rain was expected later in the day so Yorkshire would be looking for some quick wickets. The crowd was much smaller than those on the first two days with many people going back to work. Lancashire tried to make a fight of it but were all out just after lunch for 236 leaving Yorkshire to get 94 runs to win the match and stay top of the county championship table. The clouds were starting to build up and the Yorkshire openers were scoring their runs quickly and the game was over just before tea with Yorkshire winning by ten wickets.

Jack asked Jane what her plans were for the rest of the week and would she be going back into work or taking the rest of the week off. I must go back to work said Jane, my appointment book is full and I need to catch up on some paper work. Well you know where to come if you need us said Jack, you don't have to be on your own. When Jack arrived home Mary was quick to ask after Jane, she was very concerned about her good friend and needed to know if she was OK.

I told her she was welcome to come and stay with us anytime said Jack, she knows we are always here for her should she need our help. Well that's good then said Mary, Jane is a very good friend to both of us and we need to look after her when she needs us. Returning to work was not easy for Jane. She was still very upset at the way that this man had come into her life without first being referred by his doctor. He was not a nice man and he had scared her with his terrible dreams. Before her first appointment Jane made another quick phone call to her sister in Thirsk to ask how baby Lucy was. Jane was so looking forward to seeing her again and that day could not come soon enough. The day passed slowly and Jane was glad when it was time to go home. She called her taxi and looked forward to putting her feet up and having a good rest. Later that night she received a phone call from her good friend Mary asking how she was feeling, and once more asking if she would like to stay with herself and Jack for a couple of weeks. I will give it some thought she said, first I need to know if Eileen would take care of Smokey while I'm away. Jane was pleased that her friends were thinking about her. Thursday and Friday were busy days for Jane and they passed by quite quickly. Yorkshire were not playing until the following Wednesday and Jane thought about visiting her sister at the weekend. After a little more paper work Jane came out of her office and got into her taxi. She often took a taxi home in bad weather but now with all these women going missing she took a taxi home every night. A man watched as the taxi slowly pulled away, it went out of Leeds and followed the road towards Harrogate. Jane lived in a small cottage just outside Harrogate together with her cat Smokey. She had just one close neighbour who also looked after Smokey while Jane was at work. The taxi dropped Jane off at her door. She stopped for a few minutes to talk to Eileen her friend and next door neighbour who was just leaving in her car. The man following could not believe his luck, Jane was now on her own and he could now do what he needed to do. With her neighbour leaving Jane went into the cottage. The man waited until it was all clear and then pulled his car outside of Jane's front door. He gave a blast on his horn to make Jane think that it was her neighbour who had returned. Jane came out to see what she wanted but instead she had found Mr. Morris.

PART 21

He shouted at Jane to get into the car and drive. I don't drive she said and I am not getting into that car with you. Jane was terrified, she knew now that this man, the man she knew only as Mr. Morris was in fact the serial killer who was wanted by police across the country. The so called dreams he had wrote about were not dreams at all and he was just re living his killing of the missing women. I will not tell you again he shouted get in the fucking car. Still Jane refused but just then and at the wrong time Smokey her cat turned up looking to Jane for his next meal. Morris started kicking out at the cat, is this your dirty cat he shouted. Yes, it is and he is not dirty cried Jane. Morris grabbed hold of Smokey and threatened to kill him if she did not do as he asked. Jane thought the world of Smokey and would do anything she could to protect him from this killer. Alright she shouted, just put the cat down and I will get into the car. Morris dropped the cat to the ground and then kicked him so hard that he ran away. Jane started to cry shouting run Smokey run. Morris then pushed her into the car and set off at speed. It was now starting to get dark and Jane started to think about the horrible ways that the other four girls had died. She remembered him taking them to a field in the countryside which was overgrown with brambles. He would drag them screaming across the field until he reached a large stone flag covered with long grass. Morris had been strong enough to move it to one side leaving a hole which dropped down into a dark narrow passage with a terrible smell and full of rats. Jane knew in her heart of hearts that there would be no way out of this and that she was about to die too. For a moment she thought about her sister Mandy and her niece Lucy who she would never see growing up. There were also her good friends Jack Western and his wife Mary who both shared Jane's love of Yorkshire cricket. And last of all she thought about her cat Smokey who she loved very much. Who would look after him now she thought and once more she started to cry. Why are you going to kill me she said to Morris, why me? Morris looked and smiled. Because you know too much he said, YOU KNOW TOO MUCH. Later that night, when Jane's neighbour returned home, she noticed that Jane's door was still open. She stopped the car and shouted out her name, there was no reply. She got out of her car and called out again "Jane are you there" but there was no reply from inside. Eileen pushed open the door to the cottage and stepped inside. It was very cold and a fire had not been lit. She noticed Jane's handbag on the table next to her house keys but there was still no sign of Jane or Smokey. Eileen stepped back outside, it was dark now and she started shouting out her name, "JANE, ARE YOU THERE JANE" but still no reply. The following morning the police were everywhere both inside and around her cottage. There was still no sign of Jane or her cat Smokey. Police were searching woodland near to where Jane lived looking for any clues that may lead them to Jane. Four women had already gone missing and the police were taking Jane's disappearance very serious. Jane's neighbour told the police how she returned home late last night and noticed that Jane's door was still open.

She had shouted out her name but there was no sign of Jane in or outside the house. Eileen told the police how much Jane loved her cat but he was missing too. Jack and Mary Western who were both very good friends of Jane were told that she was missing after

Jack received a phone call from the police station where he had worked for many years. Jack had worked in CID and was still working on the case of the missing women in Yorkshire right up to his retirement.

Mary could not stop crying and Jack was worried about her. Poor Jane she kept saying, who would do such a terrible thing, she never hurt anyone in her whole life. And what about Mandy her sister Jack, she needs to be told that Jane is missing. I will give the station a ring now and ask about Mandy said Jack. It maybe that they do not know that Jane has a sister in Thrisk. Back in Harrogate at the cottage where Jane lived, there had been a development. A cat believed to be Jane's cat Smokey was found lying in a field at the back of Jane's cottage. The poor thing had a bad injury to his back leg and could not walk. Jane's neighbour identified him as being Smokey the cat Jane loved so much. Eileen told the police that she needed to get him to a vet who would fix his leg and give him something for the pain. She loved Smokey just as much has Jane and she told the police that she would look after him until Jane was found. Meanwhile Jack Western had contacted the station and informed them that Jane had a sister living in Thirsk. Jack was still concerned about his wife Mary, she had not taken the news about her good friend very well and was having trouble with her breathing. Jack decided it would be best to call his doctor and explain to him over the phone the reason why his wife was so upset. The doctor told Jack that he would call and see Mary later that morning after surgery. Jack too was finding it hard to take in and he remembered what Jane had told him back at the Yorkshire match with Derbyshire at Headingley. She had told him that she had become scared of one of her clients who had visited her using the name of William Morris. He had told Jane that he was having terrible dreams, dreams that were so evil that he could not talk about them. When he suddenly ended his appointments with Jane she made out her report and sent it to his doctor. A few days after this Jane received a phone call from the doctor telling her that he knew nothing about this man and had certainly not referred a man by the name of William Morris to see her. Jane had been used by this man which upset her so much that she started to cry. Jack knew that he must tell the police about this and decided to ring one of his best friends and former colleague Bill Rogers who lived in the Leeds area and worked in CID. Leave it with me said Bill and I will make sure that CID get to know about it. It might be nothing but it's certainly worth looking into. Did you say you had a name for this man Jack he asked, I do said Jack, he told Jane that his name was William Morris and that he worked as a gardener. The police visited Jane's office taking away all her files and paper work hoping that something they find might lead them to the person responsible for her disappearance. Jane's body was never found and it was thought she had become the fifth victim of a serial killer who was still unknown to the police. How many more women would have to die before the killer was caught. It was now twelve months since Jane had gone missing and Jack Weston had not been back to Headingley to watch Yorkshire. Jack had sat next to Jane at Headingley for quite a few years and he could not bring himself to go back without thinking of his dear friend Jane.

PART 22

The morning was bright and sunny and Mary was working in her garden. A young woman came through the gate with a little girl at her side.

Can I help you said Jack coming out of the house? The young woman smiled, you must be Jack she said. My name is Mandy, Jane's sister and this little girl is Lucy my daughter. Jack called out for his wife Mary, look who this is said Jack, its Jane's sister Mandy and her daughter Lucy. I thought Jane would want you to see little Lucy she said, she was always telling me what good friends you were. Mary started to cry, Jane was always talking about little Lucy and now here she was with her mum. There were lots to talk about and both Jack and Mary were holding back the tears as the memories came flooding back. Jane had talked about little Lucy every day and now here she was sat on Mary's knee. Jane would never see her grow up or hold her in her arms, she would never see her going to her first school and never be there when she got married. The three of them enjoyed coffee and biscuits while sharing their happy memories of Jane. The time came for Mandy and baby Lucy to leave, you must call again dear if ever you're in the area said Mary with a tear in her eye, and Jane would be so proud of little Lucy. Both Jack and Mary gave them both a big hug and they got up to leave. Almost forgot said Mandy taking a large brown envelope out of her bag.

Jane would want you to have these old photographs of Yorkshire Jack, thought they might be of interest to you. Jack took the envelope, still with a tear in his eye. I will treasure them forever he said and they will always remind me of happy days that we spent together at Headingley, and we will never forget our good friend Jane. The following day with Mary once again hard at work in her garden Jack decided to look through the old photographs of the Yorkshire team that Jane's sister Mandy had given him the day before. The photographs had been saved by Jane over a number of years and Mandy thought Jane would want Jack to have them. There were photographs of Yorkshire going back many years and Jane had kept them all. There was also a photograph of Jane taken with the Yorkshire captain and Jane was looking so happy and relaxed. Jack was more interested in the team photographs as many of the players had now retired. It was then that Jack picked up a photograph from a Wisden cricket magazine that made his blood run cold. Mary, Mary he shouted, take a look at this photograph. Mary came running in from the garden. Jack whatever is wrong she said. Jack told Mary to take a seat, these photographs are the ones given to me by Mandy yesterday. The photographs Jane wanted me to see and now I know why. He passed one of the photographs over to Mary asking her if she could spot anyone that she knew.

Mary took the photograph and smiled. Yes of course I can she said, look its Bill Rogers, it's your friend Bill. I wonder why Jane highlighted him and then wrote at the side Mr. Morris. Jack looked shocked, his face white. Are you feeling unwell Jack said Mary, you look quite ill. Jack looked across at Mary, his face still in shock. I need a bit of time to myself Mary, I need to think about this. Think about what she said, Jack just tell me what is wrong I need to know. I have never seen you like this before. Don't worry about this said Jack, I promise I will tell you everything when I have given it some thought. Right now I need a long walk and some fresh air. Mary was waiting on Jack when he returned home and she was in need of a few answers. I will tell you everything, Mary, but prepare yourself for a big shock. Do you remember the photograph that I asked you to look at, the one where Jane had written the name Mr. Morris at the side of Bill Rogers? Poor Jane said Mary she must have been so terrified of this man. Do you think it was this Mr. Morris that killed her Jack? And what as all this to do with Bill Rogers. He needs to be told about this before this man Mr. Morris gets away. Jack took a big breath and took hold of Mary's hand. Mary he said, his voice trembling a little, BILL ROGERS IS MR. MORRIS. Jack Western decided that his next course of action must be to return to the police station where he had worked for many years in CID and to talk with superintendent Richards who he had known for many years. Jack made a quick phone call to the station and arranged the appointment for the following day at 10am. He would be making serious allegations about a serving police officer and he needed to talk to the right man.

It was hard for both Jack and Mary to understand, Bill had been a friend to Jack for many years and to think that he might be a serial killer and the man responsible for the death of their friend Jane was hard to believe and almost out of the question. Jack went to bed that night but he hardly slept at all, he kept going over it in his mind, surely there was some mistake and Jane had got it wrong. The following morning Jack set off to the police station for his 10am appointment with superintendent Richards. He took with him the Wisden cricket photograph given to him by Jane's sister Mandy. It showed a close up photo of the Yorkshire team, and in the background the face of Bill Rogers who worked for the CID in Lancashire. At the side Jane had written the name Mr. Morris. Later that day Bill Rogers was taken into custody in Bradford and interviewed for six hours. Jane had kept records of all her meetings with Mr. Morris [known now to be Bill Rogers] together with copies of his hand written dreams. When asked if he killed Jane Wilson from Harrogate he broke down and shouted, YES, YES YES I KILLED HER AND I KILLED THE OTHER FOUR WOMEN TOO, I KILLED THEM ALL.

Later that day Bill Rogers took police officers across the field and to the passage where all the women had died. They were met with scenes of horror with some officers being physically sick and traumatised. Lights were rigged up in the passage before a team of forensics could enter. The smell was just too much and breathing masks were worn. The five women had been attacked by rats and their bodies were removed from the passage and taken away to the forensic laboratory to find out the cause of death. There was rats and blood everywhere and the smell was terrible with officers being continually sick. Jack and Mary both attended the next Yorkshire home match at Headingley staying just a short time, they were joined by Mandy and her husband John and baby Lucy. With tears in their eyes they said a prayer for Jane and placed a bunch of flowers on the seat where where she had spent so many happy days. At the end of the day Bill Rogers [Mr. Morris] had been caught out. He pleaded guilty in court to all five murders and was sentenced to spend the rest of his life behind bars. When asked why he killed Jane Wilson his Psychiatrist he replied, "SHE KNEW TOO MUCH".

ABOUT THE AUTHOR

Tony Coleman lives in Yorkshire with his wife Jean. Tony has a keen interest in sport especially cricket, football and rugby. Both himself and his wife love to travel and both love gardening.

www.ingramcontent.com/pod-product-compliance
Lightning Source LLC
Chambersburg PA
CBHW071841190726
48292CB00005B/1861